Frozen
Treats

Candy Fairies

Frozen Treats

HELEN PERELMAN

ILLUSTRATED BY
ERICA-JANE WATERS

SCHOLASTIC INC.

ISBN 978-1-338-04399-0

Text copyright © 2014 by Helen Perelman Bernstein. Illustrations copyright © 2014 by Erica-Jane Waters. All rights reserved. Published by Scholastic Inc., 557 Broadway, New York, NY 10012, by arrangement with Aladdin Paperbacks, an imprint of Simon & Schuster Children's Publishing Division. SCHOLASTIC and associated logos are trademarks and/or registered trademarks of Scholastic Inc.

The publisher does not have any control over and does not assume any responsibility for author or third-party websites or their content.

12 11 10 9 8 7 6 5 4 3 2 1   16 17 18 19 20 21

Printed in the U.S.A.   40

First Scholastic printing, May 2016

Book design by Karina Granda
The text of this book was set in New Baskerville Std.
The illustrations for this book were rendered in ink.

*For Giselle Perelman, a
sugar-tastic niece*

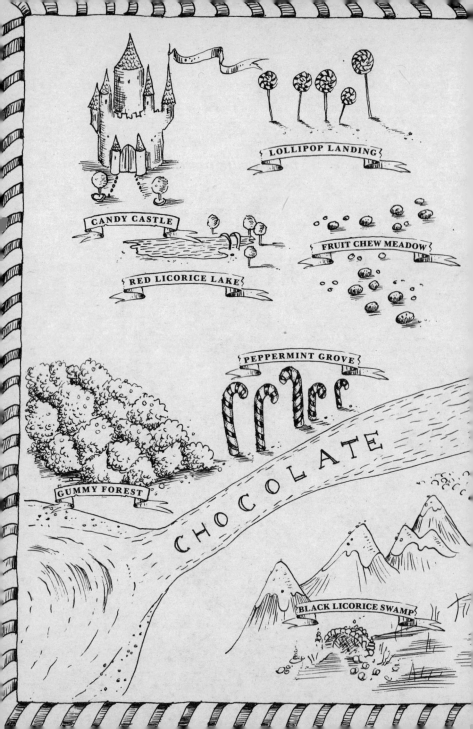

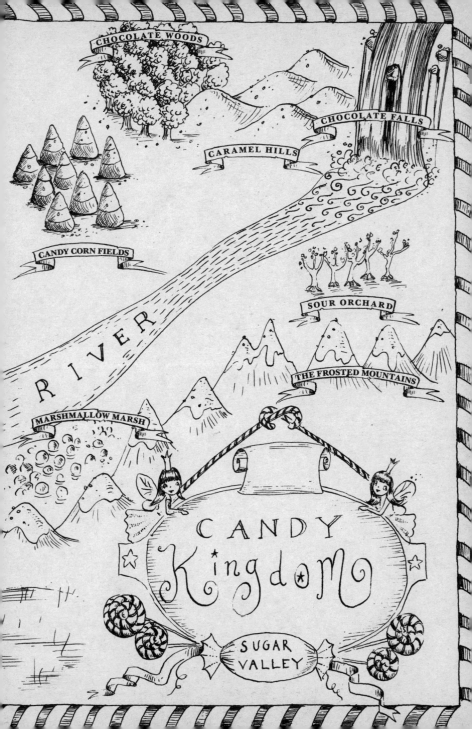

Contents

Bittersweet

Melli the Caramel Fairy licked her fingers one by one. "Mmm," she sighed. "There's nothing like the warm, gooey taste of fresh caramel." She looked over at a caramella bird perched in the tree above her. "I know you agree, right?" she asked. Melli dipped another finger into the barrel and lifted it up to the bird.

"Let me know what you think. I am trying out new recipes for a caramel sauce."

The yellow-and-white bird flew down to Melli's shoulder and gently pecked at the Candy Fairy's finger. The bird closed her eyes and flapped her wings.

Melli laughed. "I take that as a compliment!" she said.

She stirred the large wooden spoon around in the barrel once again. "I think this is just *sugar-tastic*," she told the bird. "I can't wait for Sun Dip tonight. My friends will love this sweet treat."

"We don't have to wait for tonight!" Dash the Mint Fairy called from above.

Melli looked up and was surprised to see her four Candy Fairy friends circling the barrel.

She giggled. "What are you all doing here?"

"We wanted to sample the new sauce!" Dash exclaimed. She flew near Melli. "How could we not try your dip?" The small Candy Fairy rubbed her stomach. "Any chance to try a new caramel treat!"

Raina the Gummy Fairy, Berry the Fruit Fairy, and Cocoa the Chocolate Fairy landed next to Melli.

"We wanted to come see you before you left," Cocoa added.

"Are you all packed?" Berry asked.

Melli shook her head. She was supposed to be getting ready for her trip to Ice Cream Isles, but she was too busy making the caramel sauce.

"We thought so," Cocoa said, giving Berry a knowing look. "We came to help you!"

"It's not every day a Candy Fairy gets invited to the Ice Cream Palace," Raina said proudly.

"And is asked to make something for the Summer Spectacular," Berry added.

Melli knew her friends were trying to help, but she couldn't shake being scared about her upcoming trip. She had been so excited to get the invite to Ice Cream Isles from Prince Scoop, Princess Lolli's new husband. The prince loved caramel and had asked Melli to introduce a caramel sauce at the ice cream celebration.

Melli was honored to be asked to contribute to the celebration, but she was also a little nervous about going on the journey alone.

"Is this the invitation?" Dash asked. She picked up a sugar note. "Wow, this is *so mint!*"

The invitation was a creamy vanilla color with dark chocolate lettering. She held it up for the others to see.

ICE-CREAM
ISLES

Summer Spectacular!

Dear Melli,

lolli
x

"I've never been anywhere by myself," Melli said. "Every time I've left Sugar Valley, I've been with you." She looked around at her friends. She bit her lip and tried not to cry. "What will I do without you?"

"You are only going for a few days," Berry offered.

"And Princess Lolli will be there too," Cocoa said, trying to make her friend feel better.

"Princess Lolli and Prince Scoop would not have asked you if they didn't think you could do it," Raina said.

Dash flew next to Melli. "Plus, you get to take a royal unicorn ride on Butterscotch!"

"Even with the royal unicorn, it's a long trip to Ice Cream Isles," Melli said softly. "I'm really nervous. I won't know any of the fairies." She squeezed Cocoa's hand. "I wish you all were going with me."

"We wish we could be there too," Cocoa said.

Raina opened the Fairy Code Book. "Look at these pictures," she said. "The isles are gorgeous! You are going to love it there, Melli."

The fairy friends all leaned in close to look at the pictures. The swirling landscape was breathtaking.

"I'll bet the isles are even more beautiful than in these pictures," Berry told Melli.

"Sweet Cream Harbor is full of ice cream

history," Raina said, reading the Fairy Code Book. "Swirl Island is in the middle of the harbor and is where Queen Swirl's great-grandfather, Sir Swirl, invented soft, swirling ice cream."

"Sweet ice cream scoops!" Dash exclaimed. "You are going to have a delicious time."

Cocoa reached over and turned the page. "And look at the picture of this Summer Spectacular!" she said. "It looks like everyone is having such a great time at the ice cream festival. Sure as sugar, there will be new ice cream flavors to taste! What a yummy celebration!"

"Especially with Melli's caramel sauce," Raina said, licking her finger. "Melli, this is delicious."

Melli did love looking at the pictures of the celebration.

"I'm sure you will make new friends at the Ice Cream Palace," Cocoa said. "You'll meet some really sweet Ice Cream Fairies there."

"What if they *aren't* nice?" Melli asked.

Raina put her hands on Melli's shoulders. "You are one of the kindest fairies I know," she said. "They will love you."

"Plus, you are going to give them a *sweet-sational* new ice cream sauce!" Dash exclaimed. "And you'll have to tell us everything about the Summer Spectacular and Ice Cream Isles."

"Yes!" Raina chimed in. "I wonder how they make all those glamorous ice cream floats for the parade?" She turned to another page in the Fairy Code Book and showed her friends the pictures.

"*So mint!*" Dash exclaimed. "The floats look delicious in Sweet Cream Harbor."

"You are going to have a *choc-o-rific* time," Cocoa told Melli.

"But I'm already missing you!" Melli said.

"We're here now," Dash said. "And I'd love to dip some of Cocoa's chunks of chocolate into that sauce."

Melli laughed. "Please, help yourself!" She could always count on Dash to want a snack. "I can't take this batch with me. I will need to make the sauce fresh once I am at the palace."

"No use letting all this go to waste," Dash said, rolling up her sleeves. "Those Ice Cream Fairies are so lucky to have you come visit."

As the fairies started to dip their chocolates, Cocoa pulled Melli aside. "Being away from home is hard, but you'll be too busy to miss us. You'll have to make your caramel sauce. There will be so many new things to see and do. "

Melli hoped Cocoa was right. She glanced over at the picture in the Fairy Code Book. The isles were beautiful and the Summer Spectacular was a very important event, but she also thought the place looked cold and different from Sugar Valley. She just knew that it would be a little bittersweet to be away from home.

The next morning Melli gathered up her bags. She was happy her friends had come over the night before to help her pack. Even though she was only going for a few days, her luggage looked like she was going away for a month!

As she made her way to her door, there was a knock.

Melli was surprised to see who was on her doorstep.

"Good morning, Melli!" Cocoa said. "We came to wait with you."

Melli laughed. She had thought her friends were up to something last night. "You are all so sweet," she said. "See, what am I going to do without you this week?"

Berry handed Melli a small box. "We made this for you," she told her. "This is so you remember your friends when you are away."

"Especially if you get sad," Cocoa added.

Melli didn't know what to say. She carefully opened the box. Inside was a sugarcoated ice cream cone hair clip. It was beautiful. "Hot caramel," she said. "This is *sugar-tastic*." Melli admired the fine work. She knew Berry

had used her best sugarcoated candies. She slipped the clip into her hair. "I will wear this the whole time I am away," she promised.

"And I wrote you a travel letter," Cocoa said. She handed Melli a note. "Don't read the letter until you get to the Ice Cream Palace."

"Thank you," Melli said. She slipped the note into her bag. "I will definitely read this later."

"Butterscotch should be here any minute," Dash said.

"Come wait with me out here," Melli said, pointing outside.

The fairies followed Melli to an old caramel willow tree. The five fairies sat down, but Melli was finding waiting hard. Her wings were twitching and her legs felt jumpy.

Berry began telling a story about Fruli, their Fruit Fairy friend, but Melli couldn't concentrate. She flew up above the trees. "Oh, I see Butterscotch!" Melli cried. She flew back down to her friends. "I guess it's time," she added.

Cocoa gave her a hug. "You will do great!"

"Please send a sugar fly message tonight so we know you arrived," Raina said.

"And remember every little sweet detail and everyone you meet!" Dash added.

Berry picked up one of Melli's bags and flew over to Butterscotch. "You'll be back before you know it," she said.

Melli climbed up onto Butterscotch as Raina and Berry fastened her luggage to the unicorn. She felt so small on his back. The last time he had given her a ride, she was with her four friends. She looked at the royal unicorn's wings. They were large and strong. They would get her to Ice Cream Isles in a just a couple of hours.

Cocoa flew up to Melli's side. She gave her hand a squeeze. "You'll have fun. Don't worry," she said in her ear.

Dash gave her a basket of mint candies. "You should always have some treats for a long trip," she said, smiling. "I picked all these for you."

"Thank you, Dash," Melli said. She took a deep breath. "I guess this is the good-bye part."

"Bittersweet," Cocoa said.

"Sure as sugar, you'll make us all proud," Raina said.

Berry handed Melli a soft pink wrap. "Stay warm," she told her. "And stylish."

"Thank you," Melli said, taking the wrap.

In her heart, she knew that Princess Lolli and Prince Scoop would not have asked her to come to the Summer Spectacular if they didn't think she could make the trip. She took a deep breath. "Thank you," she said again. "I will send a message when I arrive. And I'll see you soon!"

With a gallop and a giant leap, Butterscotch took off. Melli waved until she couldn't see her friends anymore. She settled into her seat and popped one of Dash's treats into her mouth. She watched all that was familiar to her fade away, and she looked out toward the horizon . . . and to Ice Cream Isles.

The steady beat of Butterscotch's wings made Melli sleepy. She wrapped Berry's shawl around her and fell asleep.

When Melli opened her eyes, she smiled. Right before her, she could see the outline of Ice Cream Isles! The isles were even more beautiful than the pictures in Raina's book. There were so many different colors and shapes. She recognized Sweet Cream Harbor, where the float parade would be during the festival, and the splendid Ice Cream Palace. The cream in

the harbor was milk white, and the wind also smelled like sweet cream.

Butterscotch began to swoop down closer to the isles. Melli took in the views and sighed. She thought of how much her friends would have loved to be with her. At that moment Melli made a promise to herself. She wouldn't spend her time missing the Candy Fairies. She was going to remember everything about Ice Cream Isles and the Summer Spectacular so she could tell them!

Butterscotch landed in the gardens of the Ice Cream Palace. The royal home was enormous. The palace was much larger than Candy Castle, and the gardens were filled with bright colors and ice cream scoop statues. All the flowering candies around the grounds were toppings for ice cream, and a rich white stream coming in from Sweet Cream Harbor created a waterfall near the front entrance. Melli knew the Candy Fairies would want to know all those details about the palace.

Melli spotted Princess Lolli and Prince Scoop. They were waiting for her! Melli was excited and nervous as she climbed off the unicorn.

"Welcome!" Prince Scoop cheered. "We are so excited to have you here for the Summer Spectacular. We know that your caramel sauce will make it an even sweeter celebration."

Princess Lolli gave Melli a warm hug. "I hope you had a good ride," she said. "It is a long way to come."

"Butterscotch is the best," Melli said. "I actually slept most of the way."

"Great," Prince Scoop said, "because we have a lot of work to do." He smiled, and Melli instantly felt at ease. "I have asked my cousins Drizzle and Fluff to help you get settled in your room at the palace," he went on. He waved at two fairies near the palace doors. "Come, I'll introduce you."

Melli followed Princess Lolli and Prince Scoop to the palace. She hoped these fairies would be nice. She felt Princess Lolli's hand squeeze hers.

"I can't believe I'm really here!" Melli exclaimed as she flew to the palace to meet the Ice Cream Fairies.

3

A Little Chilly

May I present Melli, the deliciously sweet Caramel Fairy," Prince Scoop announced. He stood on the palace steps next to Princess Lolli and two Ice Cream Fairies.

Melli felt her cheeks go as red as one of Berry's cherry lollipops.

"These are my cousins," Prince Scoop said.

"Drizzle," he added, pointing to the fairy with blond hair and chocolate swirls on her dress. "And this is Fluff," he said, putting a hand on the darker-haired fairy with a poufy white dress. "This is the first year they will be riding their own ice cream float," he added.

Melli noticed their fancy outfits and instantly felt underdressed.

Berry would love those outfits, Melli thought. *And Raina would love their names.*

Thinking of her friends made Melli a little sad, but she tried her best to smile at the two fairies standing in front of her.

"Welcome to Ice Cream Isles," Drizzle and Fluff said at the same time.

"Thank you," Melli replied. She wasn't sure what to say to these Ice Cream Fairies. In their

special outfits they seemed older than she was, and they acted so comfortable around Prince Scoop. She watched how they were chatting and laughing with their royal cousin. Melli felt a sinking feeling in her stomach. She had only been at the palace for less than five minutes, and already she was homesick and feeling out of place!

"You must be tired from your trip," Princess Lolli said, stepping closer to Melli. She put her arm around her. "Drizzle and Fluff, please show Melli to her room. She has had a long journey from Sugar Valley."

"Yes, Princess Lolli," Drizzle said.

"We'd be happy to show her," Fluff added.

"Melli, you can change and meet us down in the dining hall for dinner," Princess Lolli said.

"Thank you," Melli whispered. She couldn't wait to get up to her room. She wanted to change into her fancier dinner clothes.

Melli followed Drizzle and Fluff up the grand staircase and down a long hall lined with portraits of royal Ice Cream Fairies. They stopped in front of a door decorated with a tiny pink ice cream cone.

"How was your trip?" Drizzle asked. She opened the door for Melli and stepped inside.

"Fine, thank you," Melli said. She lowered her eyes and slipped into the room. Melli didn't know what to say. She wished Cocoa or Dash were there to start a lively conversation. There was an uncomfortable silence as they stood together.

"We'll see you around," Fluff finally said.

"Yes, thank you," Melli replied, trying to remember her manners.

When the door closed, Melli sighed. She quickly spun around and took in the beautiful palace room. There were gorgeous baskets made of the finest cotton candy, and the bed

 27

was as fluffy as a cloud of whipped cream. There were even little chocolate ice cream cones on the pillow with a note that said *Sweet Dreams.*

Melli thought of Cocoa, her Chocolate Fairy friend. She smiled as she thought about how Raina and Berry would love a room like this. Then she giggled as she imagined Dash zooming around and flopping onto the bed.

There was a large window that overlooked the palace gardens and Sweet Cream Harbor. Melli noticed how different the land looked here in Ice Cream Isles. There were no caramel or chocolate oak trees and no gummy bushes. Instead, there were cone beaches and swirls of cream. Melli noticed the sweet smell of vanilla cream again as she stood in front of the open window.

"Here I am," she said.

She flew over to her bag and unpacked her clothes. She carefully hung her dresses in the huge closet. At the bottom of her bag she found the letter from Cocoa. Melli hugged the letter and brought it over to the window seat to read.

Dear Melli,

I hope that you had a good flight over to Ice Cream Isles. You are so lucky! None of us has ever been to Ice Cream Isles, so please remember what you do, what you eat, and the special people you meet. It will be hard at first, but I am sure you will make friends. I can't wait to hear all about your time there. I miss you already!

Love, Cocoa

Melli tucked the letter back into the envelope and placed it under her pillow. If Cocoa had met Drizzle and Fluff, she would know that making friends in Ice Cream Isles was not going to be easy. Those fairies seemed a bit too cool for her, with their fancy clothes and talk of their float.

Melli put on her pink-and-red dress, which Berry had picked out for her. Berry had thought it was perfect for a royal dinner, and Melli trusted her.

There was a knock at the door. A palace guard was standing at attention.

"If you are ready for dinner, may I escort you?" he asked.

Melli's cheeks turned red once again. "Yes, thank you," she said quietly.

The guard flew next to her and brought her down to the royal dining hall. Prince Scoop and Princess Lolli were waiting for her. The long table was set with the finest sugar crystal and china. Many Royal Fairies were already seated. Everyone was very formal here at the palace. Melli wasn't sure what to do!

"Melli, you look scrumptious," Princess Lolli said, coming over to her.

"Thank you," Melli said. She was so happy to stand next to Princess Lolli. "Berry picked this outfit for me."

"You and Berry have very fine taste," Prince Scoop added. "Come, I want to show you something before dinner. My parents aren't here yet, so we have a few moments."

The three of them flew outside to the garden, where the view of Sweet Cream Harbor was even more spectacular than it had been from her bedroom window.

Melli's eyes were wide with excitement. "This is even more *sugar-tastic* than the draw-·ings in the Fairy Code Book!"

The royal couple laughed.

"The harbor is where the Summer Spec-tacular will happen," Prince Scoop told Melli. "In a few days this waterway will be filled with ice cream floats. And the ice cream festival is over on Swirl Island."

"A new flavor is served every year," Princess Lolli added. "It's my favorite part!"

Prince Scoop pointed to a small island across the harbor. "That is Swirl Island, where everyone will taste your caramel sauce."

"Oh my," Melli said, taking it all in.

"Don't worry," Princess Lolli said. "Everyone is going to love your caramel."

 33

Melli smiled at Princess Lolli.

"Let's head in for dinner," Prince Scoop said.

As they walked back to the dining hall, Melli noticed a few large barrels of different sauces lined up outside in the garden.

"There is an empty barrel for your caramel sauce," Prince Scoop said, pointing to a container at the end. "I can't wait for you to fill it up!"

"The sauce needs a Caramel Fairy's touch," Princess Lolli added. "The fairies here have been having trouble getting the sauce just right."

Melli smiled. "That's why I'm here. Thank you again for inviting me."

"Come this way," Prince Scoop replied, holding the door open. As they entered the dining hall, Melli saw that King Cone and Queen Swirl were already at the table. Prince Scoop introduced Melli to the royal couple.

Melli curtsied. "Thank you for inviting me here," she said. "It is so nice to see you again after Prince Scoop and Princess Lolli's wedding." She had practiced that curtsy and line a few hundred times!

"We're happy to have you here," King Cone stated.

"We hope you enjoy your time during your stay," Queen Swirl added.

Melli remembered from the wedding that Prince Scoop's parents were very formal. Melli nodded and took her seat next to Drizzle and Fluff, who were deep in conversation. They didn't seem to notice Melli one bit.

There were many fairies around the table, and they were all dressed so beautifully.

Berry would love this! Melli thought.

Princess Lolli was on the other side of the room, and Melli wished she could be next to her. Then she remembered her promise to herself. She didn't want to be sad. So what if the fairies next to her weren't speaking to her and were giving her the freeze? She was eating with the king and queen! Melli wanted to go back to Sugar Valley with wonderful, sweet stories to tell her friends.

As the meal began Melli searched for something to say to the Ice Cream Fairies next to her. She turned toward Fluff just as the server was placing a bowl of chilled soup in front of her. Melli's arm hit the dish, and she

almost made the serving fairy spill the soup! She faced forward and didn't move. Everyone else at the table seemed to know exactly what to say and do. Melli tried to enjoy her soup, but she was too busy making sure she was being proper and not making mistakes.

When the serving fairy had moved on, Melli looked up. She realized the royal family hadn't seemed to notice her mistakes. In fact, no one seemed to notice her at all!

Melli couldn't shake the feeling that her first trip ever by herself was going to be a bit cold.

4

Surprising Sauce

After dinner Princess Lolli and Melli flew up the long palace staircase to their rooms.

"I am glad that you're here," Melli said when they were alone in the hallway.

Princess Lolli smiled. "I'm glad that *you're* here!" she said. "Scoop has been talking about bringing caramel sauce to Ice Cream Isles for a long time. The Summer Spectacular is the perfect time for it. And I can't think of anyone more perfect for the job than you."

"Yes, the ice cream festival does seem like just the right occasion," Melli said. But she started to worry a bit about actually getting the sauce perfect here. Everything about Ice Cream Isles seemed to be different.

Princess Lolli stopped in front of Melli's door. "Ah, here is your room. I *still* get lost in these halls," she said.

Melli realized that the palace was still new to Princess Lolli. She and Prince Scoop hadn't been married for long.

"Do you miss Candy Castle?" Melli asked.

"I do," Princess Lolli said. "But now that Scoop and I are married, it's nice to spend time in both places." She smiled at Melli. "Do you have everything you need for tonight?" she asked.

"Yes, thank you," Melli said. "I want to send my friends a sugar note and then go to sleep. I need to start on the sauce early tomorrow morning."

"Very well," Princess Lolli said as she headed out the door. "Sweet dreams, Melli."

Melli wrote a quick sugar fly message. She let the Candy Fairies know that she had arrived safely at the palace. She left out meeting Drizzle and Fluff. She didn't know what to say about them. She didn't want to write *I met two Ice Cream Fairies. I nearly knocked*

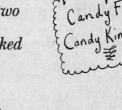

over a fairy serving soup, and then no one talked to me. I was so embarrassed. Melli thought it best to leave all that out for now.

Settling into her royal bed, Melli thought she would have a hard time falling asleep. But when she put her head down on the pillow, she fell asleep in seconds.

The sun streamed into Melli's room early the next morning. She realized that she had not closed the curtains on the large bedroom window. But she didn't mind the early wake-up. She ate a quick breakfast of fresh fruit treats and then was on her way. She had a lot of work to do.

Melli flew out to the garden area where Prince Scoop had pointed out the barrels of sauces. To her surprise, Prince Scoop and Drizzle were there.

"Good morning!" Prince Scoop called. "You're up very early."

"Good morning, Prince Scoop. Good morning, Drizzle. I wanted to get a head start," Melli said. She thought about Dash and how bold and minty she could be. She put a smile on her face.

"Hi," Drizzle said quietly.

Prince Scoop clapped his hands together. "Drizzle, can you help Melli and show her where our supplies are? Melli, maybe Drizzle can help you with the caramel sauce. You two can work together."

Melli wasn't too sure about that. When people worked together, they needed to talk to each other! At least, that's the way it was in Sugar Valley.

"I have some morning appointments about the parade, but I'll check on you two later," Prince Scoop said as he flew off.

Once Prince Scoop had left, there was an awkward silence between Drizzle and Melli.

But then Drizzle spoke. "I once tried to make caramel sauce," she said. "I got stuck near the end of the recipe. It was too thick to drizzle or to use as a dip."

"Hmm," Melli said. "Did you melt the caramel blocks first?"

"Caramel blocks?" Drizzle asked. She wrinkled up her nose. "What are those?"

"They're the best way to melt the caramel for a sauce," Melli replied. She opened up her bag and dropped a few large bricks of caramel into the barrel. She felt Drizzle's eyes on her.

"I've never seen caramel like that before," Drizzle said. "We usually just get small chips or scraps."

Smiling, Melli lit the fire under the barrel and began to stir. If there was one thing she knew about, it was caramel sauce. Her wings straightened as she swirled the mixture. Slowly she added more caramel. She showed Drizzle how she found that combining the dark and light caramel flavors made the sweetest sauce.

"Does a Caramel Fairy ever run out of caramel blocks?" Drizzle asked, her eyes wide.

"No," Melli said with a giggle. "She can keep making more! Just some pure sugar and Caramel Fairy magic!"

Drizzle laughed. "Lucky you," she said. "Ever since Prince Scoop met Princess Lolli, he has been talking about caramel. And all the Ice Cream Fairies couldn't wait to taste caramel sauce on ice cream sundaes!"

The two took turns stirring the caramel. Maybe because Melli loved making caramel, or maybe because Drizzle was busy telling a story about Prince Scoop when he was younger, the morning passed quickly.

Drizzle leaned over Melli's barrel. "That smells delicious!"

"Well, now you can try it for yourself," Melli said. "She lifted up the paddle and put some sauce into a bowl. "Maybe dip one of those chocolate chips and see what you think."

Drizzle took a chocolate chunk from a basket

and lowered it into the bowl. The caramel color was just right, and Melli held her breath as Drizzle put the coated treat in her mouth.

"Sweet cream!" Drizzle cried.

"Oh no!" Melli said, alarmed. "Is something wrong?"

Drizzle laughed. "No, this is just so good!" She licked her lips. "And it will be such a yummy topping for ice cream!"

Melli grinned. Maybe Drizzle wasn't so cold after all.

Just then Prince Scoop returned with Fluff by his side. He looked into the barrel. "You have been busy this morning," he said. "Looks like we've finally got some caramel sauce for the Spectacular! Please join us for lunch when you finish up."

Melli's wings fluttered, and her feet lifted slightly off the ground.

But then she saw Drizzle talking and laughing with Fluff and looking her way.

Are they laughing at me? Melli wondered. *I thought we were having fun.*

She felt a chill in the air and wished she had Berry's wrap with her.

As Prince Scoop flew away a sugar fly landed on Melli's shoulder. She took the note and saw that it was from Berry. She was so happy to get a note from one of the Candy Fairies. "We hope you are having a *sugartastic* time and making new friends. We miss you," she read. Melli sent a sugar fly message back home, but this time she didn't hold back. *I've made the sauce, but not friends.*

Everyone is so cold! she wrote. *I miss you all.*

Melli looked over again and saw Drizzle and Fluff walking together into the palace. Why didn't they wait for her or ask her to join them?

Would lunch be just as awful as dinner had been last night? Melli didn't have much of an appetite at all.

CHAPTER 5

Sinking Feeling

Having no Candy Fairy friends with her wasn't the only thing Melli wasn't used to at Ice Cream Isles. She also wasn't used to all the fancy meals and different foods at the Ice Cream Palace. She wished she could have some fruit nectar or chocolate soup outside and continue with her work. But since she was Princess Lolli and Prince Scoop's guest staying at the palace, she had to go along with their customs and have grand meals in the royal dining hall.

On her third day Melli was already tired of the formal meals, and especially the silent treatment from Drizzle and Fluff. Yesterday's lunch and last night's dinner were no different from the first night's meal. She had sat and watched Drizzle and Fluff chatter and laugh while she had felt out of place. Even though she'd had a good time with Drizzle making the caramel, in the dining hall she felt invisible. And she didn't want to bother Princess Lolli, who looked very busy herself with entertaining all the royal guests around the table.

So with the Summer Spectacular happening

the next day, she decided to focus on the job she had come to do and spent the morning preparing another barrel of caramel sauce. She left the barrel under the shade of a large chocolate willow tree to cool while she went back to the palace for lunch. The tree reminded her of Cocoa and all the time they'd spent in Chocolate Woods together. The tree was not as large as the chocolate oaks that grew in the woods in Sugar Valley, but the fragrant tree made her think of her friends . . . and home.

Inside the royal dining hall, Melli saw that most of the fairies were already seated. At each of these festive meals, the queen and king invited royal and honored guests to eat with them. Melli saw Drizzle at the far end of the table. The seat next to her was empty.

"Don't dip your wings in syrup yet," she could hear her friend Berry say to her. Was Drizzle smiling at her? Melli smiled at Drizzle and flew over to her.

But as Melli reached the seat next to Drizzle, Fluff slipped into the chair!

"Hi, Fluff!" Drizzle said brightly. The two cousins quickly started chatting and never looked up to see Melli fluttering all alone.

Melli thought she had caught Drizzle's eye. Had Drizzle not seen her? Or had she seen her and called Fluff over instead?

The service bell to begin the meal rang. Many palace fairies holding silver platters filled the hall and began to place the dishes on the table.

Oh no! Where was she going to sit? The

Royal Fairies were not supposed to start eating until everyone was seated! Melli looked up and down the table and then spotted a open seat—next to Queen Swirl! It was hard enough sitting next to Drizzle and Fluff, but Queen Swirl? What would they talk about? Melli sat down and lowered her head. She didn't want anyone to see how nervous she was . . . most of all the queen.

Even though Melli was hungry, she found eating very difficult. She was trying so hard to remember all her manners and say and do everything correctly. Princess Lolli was not at lunch, and Prince Scoop was speaking to his father and some other fairies at the opposite end of the table.

Melli wanted to slouch her wings, but she

didn't dare! She wanted the queen to like her and to report back to Princess Lolli that she had been a well-mannered guest. Being so proper at these meals was exhausting! Melli tried her best and smiled and nodded when the queen spoke to her. She didn't dare slurp her fruit nectar!

Finally the ice cream dessert was served. Melli politely excused herself from the table. She was about to fly out of the dining hall in tears, when Prince Scoop stood up to make an announcement. She sat down as the prince spoke to the fairies.

"I would like to ask that all fairies working on their floats get them in the water by tomorrow morning," he said. "We'll have a practice run first thing."

The queen turned to Melli. "Melli, my dear,

 56

have you been assigned a float?" she asked.

Melli shook her head. She wasn't even sure what being assigned a float meant.

"Drizzle and Fluff," Queen Swirl called, "do you have room for another fairy on your float?"

"Oh, that is not necessary, Queen Swirl," Melli said quickly. "I can just watch."

The queen stood up. "Nonsense!" she said. "You need to be on a float to experience the Spectacular. Why, I recall my first Summer Spectacular," she went on. She fanned her face with waffle cone fan. "To ride on a float in Sweet Cream Harbor is just divine."

Melli watched Drizzle and Fluff. There was no way they could deny the queen. Melli's wings twitched. She wished with all her heart that she had the magic to disappear at that moment!

"I don't want to cause any trouble," Melli said softly.

"This is no trouble," Queen Swirl replied. She looked at Drizzle and Fluff. "What do you two say?"

"Yes, Aunt Swirl," Fluff replied. "Melli can ride with us."

Fluff's words came out as sticky as the caramel sauce cooling outside. Melli didn't know much about the floats in the harbor, but she could tell when a fairy didn't want to do something.

"Please, Queen Swirl," Melli said. "I'll be fine watching."

"No," the queen said, "you'll ride with Drizzle and Fluff. It's settled." She sat back in her chair. "You'll love the ride, Melli. It's one of the sweetest days in the Isles."

Melli nodded. She was afraid that if she opened her mouth to speak, she might start crying. She felt her face turning red, and she rushed out of the room.

She had a sinking feeling that riding in the float with Drizzle and Fluff was a bad idea. Was coming to Ice Cream Isles in the first place a bad idea too?

CHAPTER
6

Sticky Situation

Melli left the palace and flew out to Sweet Cream Harbor. Now that the caramel sauce was finished and cooling, she could take a break from the work—and those cool Ice Cream Fairies.

Maybe I can leave now—before the Spectacular, Melli thought. *The caramel sauce is done.*

No one will even miss me or know I'm gone.

But then she remembered her friends and how they were counting on her to tell them about the Summer Spectacular, the newest ice cream flavors, and the colorful floats.

She *couldn't* leave.

The smell and the beautiful scene from the purple sandy beach at Sweet Cream Harbor calmed Melli. She found a smooth rock and sat down to enjoy the view . . . and being alone.

There were a few Spectacular floats bobbing in the water. Some Ice Cream Fairies were putting finishing touches on their floats or anchoring them in the harbor. There were some very fancy ones with lots of decorations. Each float looked like a delicious dessert with colorful trimmings. Melli was amazed at the whipped cream and candy toppings. She took off her shoes and dug her feet down into the cool purple sand. She longed to be on the red sugar sand beach at Red Licorice Lake. In a few hours her friends would gather at Licorice Lake for Sun Dip. She felt a lump in her stomach.

Melli wrote a sugar fly note. *I miss you all very much,* she scribbled and then paused. *I haven't made any friends because the Ice Cream Fairies are like Frozen Fairies.* Again she felt bad about sending sad thoughts, but she folded the note and sent it away.

Since her friends weren't there, Melli tried to imagine what they would say about this float situation. She was sure that Dash would be frustrated on the slow-moving ride and that Berry would love the attention of being in a parade. Cocoa and Raina would be excited about decorating the float.

How was she going to get out of riding the float with Drizzle and Fluff? Now that Queen Swirl had gotten involved, it would be hard not to go. Melli watched the waves and saw how the tide was rolling in closer to her. Now the cold water was just reaching her toes.

All of sudden Melli heard a loud cry. She flew up from the rock and looked around.

"Hello? Where are you?" Melli called. "Are you all right?" She spun around in the air, looking for the creature that had called to her. Down by the water's edge she saw a white shape in the sand. It looked like an animal.

"Hot caramel!" Melli exclaimed. She saw a

white seal struggling. The animal was trying to free herself before the tide rolled in.

Melli flew out to her and saw a cone stuck on one of the seal's flippers. "You sweet thing," she cried. "You can't swim."

With each wave, the water around the seal got deeper. If the tide came in and the seal was still stuck, the poor animal might drown if she couldn't swim. Melli had no time to lose.

Melli wished her friends were there to help. Raina would have the Fairy Code Book on hand and recite a story that would be helpful. Dash and Berry would be quick to come up with a plan, and Cocoa would be brave and daring.

Melli had to act fast—and alone.

"Hold on," she said. She looked closely and saw that the cone had a thick layer of marshmallow topping on the edge. The cone was holding her flipper down in the sand. No wonder she couldn't move.

"You are lucky that I am a Caramel Fairy," Melli told the seal. "I know all about how to deal with stickiness."

The seal relaxed a little with this news, but the water was still rising fast.

And I thought I was in a sticky situation, Melli thought. She smiled and tried to stay calm so the seal wouldn't worry.

The truth was, Melli *was* concerned. She didn't have much time before the water would get too deep for her to help. And she had to be extra-careful with her wings. If her wings got wet, she would not be able to fly, and that would be dangerous for both her and the seal.

"Hold on," Melli said. She tugged the cone with all her might, but it would not budge.

The seal whimpered and looked up at Melli with the saddest eyes.

"I'll get it this time," she said. Melli took out some powdered sugar from her pocket. She sprinkled the powder while the tide pulled back. "This should help," she told the seal.

Within seconds of a large rolling wave, Melli was able to pull the cone off the seal's flipper. She hurled the sticky cone toward the shore. She would throw it out after she knew the seal was safe.

The seal dove underwater and joyously flipped her flipper. Melli followed the animal to a rocky area where they both could rest on a high ledge away from the rising water.

"What's your name?" Melli asked.

The seal dipped her hind flippers in the water and barked.

"Dips?" Melli guessed. She laughed. "That sounds like a good name for a seal who lives in Ice Cream Isles."

Dips barked again, and Melli was pleased to have made at least one friend in this kingdom. Eager to talk to someone, Melli told the seal about the caramel sauce and about being far from home without her Candy Fairies.

Dips nestled her cool, wet nose in Melli's hand. Even though they didn't speak the same language, Melli knew Dips was grateful for her help.

"Sweet caramel sauce," Melli said. "I'm so glad we met."

Dips clapped her front flippers together.

Melli giggled. "Yes," she said, grinning. "You helped me, too. You're the first true friend that I've found here." She slipped Dips a caramel from her pocket. "Thanks, Dips. You made me feel much better."

Together, Melli and Dips watched from the beach as the sun dipped down below the horizon. While it wasn't the same as watching the sun slide behind the Frosted Mountains

in Sugar Valley, the sky was a gorgeous swirl of scrumptious colors.

"Sure as sugar, Sun Dip with a good friend is always sweet," Melli said with a sigh. She hugged Dips, and they sat watching the sun slip out of sight.

CHAPTER 7

Cherry on a Sundae

After Sun Dip, Melli returned to the palace gardens. She was sad to say good-bye to Dips, but she had to check on the caramel sauce one last time before dinner and tomorrow's festivities. To her surprise, Drizzle and Fluff were there. And it looked like they were waiting for her!

"Oh sweet sprinkles, she's here!" Drizzle cried. She flew up to Melli as soon as she saw her.

"Where have you been?" Fluff asked, trailing behind.

Melli wasn't sure if the fairies were asking because they cared or because they were mad. She shrugged. "I was at Sweet Cream Harbor," she replied.

"We've been waiting for you," Drizzle said.

"Why? Is the caramel sauce all right?" Melli asked, concerned.

Drizzle said, "That's not why we're here, Melli."

"What do you mean?" Melli looked from Drizzle to Fluff and then back to Drizzle. "What's going on? What's wrong? What do you want?" Melli grew more and more upset.

Slowly lifting her head, she knew there was no way she could hide the fact that she had started to cry. Meeting Dips at Sun Dip was nice and she was grateful to be here, but she was ready to leave. She touched her ice cream cone clip in her hair. "I'm sorry," she said. "I miss my home."

Fluff handed Melli a handkerchief. "It must be hard to be so far from home." She guided Melli over to a bench to sit down.

"You aren't what I thought you'd be like," Drizzle said. She joined them on the bench. "At first I thought you were so formal. Fluff and I thought *you* didn't want to be friends with *us*. You sat with the princess and then the queen . . . and you sounded so proper."

"Proper?" Melli asked. "Did you see when I

almost spilled my soup over the fairy serving the meal at my first dinner here? And how I barely spoke at all during meals because I was so nervous?"

"You didn't look nervous," Fluff said. "You looked just like one of the royals!"

"Yesterday I wanted to sit with you at lunch," Melli said, "but there were no more seats near you. Fluff sat down next to you before I had a chance."

"Oh," Drizzle said. "I just thought you didn't want to sit next to me."

"I didn't think that *you* wanted *me* to sit there," Melli told her. "And now the queen has practically ordered you to have me ride in the parade with you two." She wiped her eyes and sniffled.

"Well, *that* is the problem," Drizzle said. She looked over at Fluff.

Melli's mouth fell open. So these fairies *really* didn't want to be friends with her! Melli stood up. How sour could these Ice Cream Fairies be?

"No, that is not what I meant!" Drizzle said quickly. "It's not that it's a problem if you ride with us. It's just—"

"Don't worry about it," Melli said, cutting her off. She didn't want to hear any excuses. And she definitely didn't want to ride on a float with fairies who didn't want to be her friends. She fluttered her wings, ready to fly back to the palace.

"The truth is, we haven't finished our float for the parade!" Fluff blurted out. "We haven't even put it in the water! It's our first year building a float. And if we don't get it right, it might be our last."

"And the parade is tomorrow!" Drizzle added. "And now Queen Swirl is definitely going to notice since she is expecting to see *you* on *our* float!"

Melli thought back on her time in Ice Cream Isles. She wondered how differently Drizzle and Fluff had experienced the same events that she had. . . . Had she seemed snobby? And superproper? She was just so nervous and shy.

"Come, we'll show you our float," Drizzle said. She took Melli's hand, and the three fairies flew to Sweet Cream Harbor.

There were a few mints lighting up the work area. Melli bent down to examine the float.

"The sauce is too heavy," Melli said. "This will never float. You could sprinkle some caramel flakes or use just a splash of caramel. That should take some of the weight off the float."

"Would you help us finish?" Drizzle asked.

Before Melli could answer, Fluff started to

speak. "We're really sorry," she said. "Maybe we can start over. Drizzle and I had the wrong idea about you. I think that we'd make a good team."

Melli thought that Fluff was a lot like Dash. She was too quick to speak at times—and could be a little minty. Melli took a deep breath and looked at the two fairies standing in front of her. Maybe she had been wrong about them, too. Now Drizzle and Fluff didn't seem so sour. They were just having a big problem and didn't know how to solve it.

Melli rolled up her sleeves. "We don't have all that much time," she said. "There are already a few floats in the harbor. Maybe if we work quickly, we can be ready for tomorrow."

"Melli, you are the sweetest," Drizzle gushed. "I'm sorry if your time here has been sticky."

"I'm glad that the three of us will be working together," Fluff said. "We just need a plan."

"This is what my friends and I do in Sugar Valley," Melli explained. "If we work together, we'll be able to get this done . . . and maybe even win a float prize."

"Well, that would be the cherry on the ice cream float!" Fluff exclaimed.

"You know," Melli said, thinking out loud, "I have a great idea to make the float extra-special."

"How?" Drizzle asked.

"Come with me. Quickly!" she said. She waved for Drizzle and Fluff to follow her and they took off into the darkening sky.

CHAPTER 8

Sweetness Afloat

Melli led the way toward Sweet Cream Harbor. There was a soft purple swirl on the dark horizon. She looked back over her shoulder. Drizzle and Fluff were keeping up with her speed, but they looked confused.

"Almost there!" Melli called.

"Where are we going?" Drizzle asked.

Fluff flew closer to Melli. "Are we going to Sweet Cream Harbor?"

"You'll see," Melli replied. She dipped down to the right and headed for the water.

The moon was half full, giving just enough light to see. The three fairies flew lower, toward the rocky beach.

"Let's go to the edge of the water," Melli called. She swooped down to the beach and the lapping waves. Now that the tide had gone out, the beach was wide. Melli landed on a soft patch of purple sand. "I watched Sun Dip from here today," she told the Ice Cream Fairies. "It was *sugar-tastic*. The colors were delicious."

"Who are we meeting here?" Drizzle asked. "Or waiting for?"

"No one is here," Fluff said, spinning around.

"I have to call her," Melli replied. She flew out over the water. Even though the light was dim, Melli searched the waters. "Dips!" she called. "Dips, come to the shore by the rocks!" she shouted.

"Who is Dips?" Fluff asked when Melli returned. "Another Candy Fairy?"

Melli laughed. "No, not a Candy Fairy, but a very sweet friend. Come, let's go wait over here." She flew to the rocks and sat down. "She'll be here soon."

Drizzle and Fluff shared a worried look as they sat down next to Melli. Melli just smiled as she looked out into the harbor. She knew her friend would come. And she hoped that when she did, Dips would agree to her plan.

"It is so pretty here," Melli said.

"Sweet Cream Harbor has a lot of ice cream history," Drizzle told her. "This is the site of the big swirl." She stood up and pointed to a very large ice cream swirl off in the distance. "Do you see Swirl Island?"

Melli thought about how Raina had read about Swirl Island in the Fairy Code Book. She wished her friends were with her now to see the beautiful swirled island.

"There's a large statue of Queen Swirl's great-grandfather, Sir Swirl, on the island," Drizzle went on. "The ice cream festival is held there to honor him every year. No trip to Ice Cream Isles is complete without a stop at Swirl Island."

Fluff licked her lips. "And Swirl Island still has the best ice cream flavors," she said.

 85

"If only we could get our float moving," Drizzle said. "Then you could be part of the big float parade."

Fluff and Drizzle sighed.

"The float will move," Melli said. "I can almost promise you that!"

Just then there was a splash to the left of the rock where they were sitting.

Dips had come!

The little white seal peeked her head out of the water.

Melli leaned over the rock to greet her furry pal. "Dips, these are my friends Drizzle and Fluff," she said. "We've come because we need your help."

"How do you know a Sweet Cream Harbor seal?" Drizzle asked, amazed.

"Wow," Fluff said. Her eyes gleamed as she looked over at the seal. "I've never seen a seal so close up before!"

Melli reached out to Dips. "Oh, we're old friends," she said. "This afternoon I helped Dips out of a sticky situation."

Dips jumped out of the water and hit Melli's hand gently with her flipper.

"What would you think if we had this sweet seal pull the float?" Melli asked. "I bet no one else has ever thought of that. It would be spectacular, right?"

"A real frozen treat!" Drizzle exclaimed. "Sweetness afloat!"

"We'll be the hit of the float parade," Fluff added. "You're brilliant, Melli!" She looked down at Dips. "But will Dips be able to pull the float? Would she want to?"

"What do you say, Dips?" Melli asked, grinning. "Will you be part of our team?"

Drizzle, Fluff, and Melli held hands as Dips dove underwater. They weren't sure what the seal was doing.

But then Dips leaped up, triumphant. She slapped the water with a hind flipper, playfully splashing the fairies.

"I think that is an enthusiastic yes," Melli said, wiping the spray of water off her face.

"Triple scoop!" Fluff said.

"Now that Dips has agreed," Melli said, "we need to finish the float so that she can pull it."

"We'll meet you back here first thing

tomorrow morning," Drizzle told Dips. "We will have to prepare a light sauce and maybe a sprinkle of colored sugar."

"Sounds perfect," Melli said.

Before they left, a tiny sugar fly flew to Melli's shoulder. The fly's wings tickled her face.

"Someone is trying to get your attention," Fluff said, giggling.

Melli opened the note. Her eyes widened. "This is from Princess Lolli!" she cried. "Oh hot caramel, we missed dinner! I hope she isn't angry."

"That doesn't sound like Princess Lolli, to get angry about that," Drizzle said.

Melli held up the note.

"No," she said. She continued reading. "Wait, she says it is urgent that we come to the palace."

"What's wrong?" Drizzle asked. "Did she say why?" She leaned over to look at the sugar fly note.

Melli shook her head. "She doesn't say. The note only asks us to return to the palace immediately. If Princess Lolli says to come, we had better hurry!"

Dips slapped her hind flippers down on the water as the three fairies raced back to the palace.

What could be wrong at the palace? Melli hoped that Princess Lolli and Prince Scoop were all right. She flapped her wings even faster.

Just when things were going well, she thought.

9

Messy Milk

When the Ice Cream Palace came into view, Melli saw Prince Scoop waiting outside the large front gates. She was shocked to see who was with him. She squinted her eyes to make sure she was seeing correctly. She dipped down and flew faster.

Prince Scoop was talking to Melli's Candy Fairy friends!

"Hot caramel!" Melli shouted as she landed.

There was a burst of screams, followed by lots of hugs and laughter.

"What are you doing here?" Melli asked. She gave Cocoa a tight squeeze. "When did you get here?"

"Isn't this *choc-o-rific*?!" Cocoa exclaimed. "We just arrived!"

Berry and Raina took Melli's hands. "We're so happy to see you!" they said at the same time.

"And *sooooo* happy to be here in Ice Cream Isles!" Dash added.

Melli laughed. She couldn't believe her

friends were actually standing in front of her at the Ice Cream Palace!

"I knew this was going to be a sweet surprise," Princess Lolli said. "I wanted all you Candy Fairies to experience the Summer Spectacular and the ice cream float parade. Butterscotch flew them in for the celebration tomorrow."

"And for Melli's *sugar-tastic* caramel sauce!" Dash added.

There was so much chattering and shrieking that Prince Scoop clapped his hands for quiet. "Come," he said. "Let's go inside for a snack. I am sure our travelers are hungry." He led the group of fairies toward the palace doors.

"I'm so sorry that Drizzle, Fluff, and I missed dinner tonight," Melli said.

"Were you working on a float?" Princess Lolli asked.

"I remember some late nights when I was making my first float," Prince Scoop said.

Melli was relieved that the princess and prince understood. She looked back at Drizzle and Fluff. But they were standing awkwardly by the gate.

"You go inside with Princess Lolli and Prince Scoop," Melli told Dash, Cocoa, Berry, and Raina. "I'll be right in."

Her friends went inside the palace while Melli flew over to Drizzle and Fluff.

"Those are your Candy Fairy friends from Sugar Valley?" Drizzle asked.

"Yes," Melli replied. She realized she had not introduced her new Ice Cream Isles friends to her Candy Fairy friends. "Please come inside to the dining hall. I didn't get a chance to introduce you," she said. "I'd like you to meet one another."

Fluff said, "We really have to work on the float. You go ahead."

Melli took their hands. "No," she said. "I want you to meet my friends. We can finish the float later. We'll work quickly." She smiled at Drizzle and Fluff. "Please?"

Drizzle and Fluff exchanged a glance. Melli was relieved when they both nodded and agreed to go with her.

But when Melli introduced Drizzle and Fluff to the Candy Fairies, they were very quiet. The Candy Fairies were sitting together at one end of the table and making no move to get up or talk to the Ice Cream Fairies. Melli sat awkwardly in the middle.

"Are those the Frozen Fairies?" Cocoa whispered to Melli.

"No," Melli said quickly. "Please don't call them that. It was a misunderstanding." She looked over at the other end of the table. She knew that Drizzle and Fluff had noticed the whispering was about them. "Please, Cocoa," she whispered. "Be nice."

"I will be," Cocoa said, staring at the Ice Cream Fairies. "As nice as they were to you."

Melli sighed. She should never have sent those sugar fly messages! She knew she should have thought first. Now her friends had the wrong impression of Drizzle and Fluff. And it was all her fault.

Melli twirled her ice cream scoops around in her bowl. She didn't feel like eating. The two colors, strawberry pink and creamy vanilla, mixed together and made a milky mess.

Princess Lolli came over to Melli once the dishes had been cleared. "Melli, I heard how wonderful you were to Dips," she said. "You saved her. We are all very grateful that you were there to help."

"Dips is so sweet," Melli said. "I'm glad that I could help. And now she is going to help us."

"Oh?" Princess Lolli said. She raised her eyebrows high.

Melli grinned. "We have a secret surprise!" she said. She looked over at Drizzle and Fluff.

"What's that?" Cocoa asked.

Melli didn't know that Cocoa had been

listening. "Oh, you'll see tomorrow," Melli told her. "You should rest up tonight. Tomorrow is going to be the most spectacular Summer Spectacular!"

Cocoa looked at Melli and shrugged. "If I didn't know better," she said, "I would think that you were trying to get rid of us."

"No, no," Melli said. "I just . . ."

Drizzle finished her sentence for her. "She just has work to do tonight."

Melli saw the surprised looks on her friends' faces. Princess Lolli stepped in and told the other Candy Fairies to follow her upstairs. "I'm sure Melli will join you shortly," she said sweetly.

"Yes," Melli added quickly. She was grateful to Princess Lolli for taking her friends to their rooms.

She fluttered her wings and tried to shake the awkward, sticky feeling. As she flew to Sweet Cream Harbor with Drizzle and Fluff, she hoped that the other fairies would understand.

Once at the harbor, the three fairies pulled their float out of the shed and started to work. It was late and the light was dim, but they knew what to do. They scraped the heavy sauce off and put a on light, fluffy layer of marshmallow.

"I think my friends have the wrong impression of you two," Melli said as they worked.

"What do you mean?" Fluff asked.

Melli sprinkled rainbow sugar crystals around the float. "Well, when I first got here I sent a sugar fly note about how things here were a little chilly." Melli looked away. She wished she could take back those words.

"Oh," Drizzle said. She sat down. "That might explain the frosty stares at our introduction."

"I'm really sorry," Melli said. "I will explain everything tomorrow. I want them to get to know you. I want all of us to be friends."

At last, the three fairies finished up the float. They were tired and had smudges of marshmallow from ear to ear.

"This is delicious!" Fluff cried. "And Dips is going to be an extra-sweet addition."

Melli admired their work. "You know," she said, "this seems much bigger than the other floats I saw in the harbor today."

Together, the three fairies pushed the float back into the shed so it would be a surprise the next morning.

"The float *is* much bigger. Now I'm really glad we have Dips to pull it," Drizzle said as she pushed.

Fluff snapped her fingers. "Maybe we could make this a double-scoop float," she said. "Then we could have *more* fairies on it.

"My friends don't expect to be *in* the Spectacular," Melli said, smiling. "They think they are just watching from the palace beach. It will be a delicious surprise. Would you both be okay with that?"

Fluff and Drizzle shared a smile. "The more the merrier," Fluff said.

"Super sundae!" Drizzle exclaimed.

Melli grinned. She couldn't wait to tell her friends!

10

Frozen Treat Ending

The morning of the Summer Spectacular, Melli woke up with the sunrise. She dressed and hurried out to Sweet Cream Harbor. She felt bad sneaking off while her friends slept, but she left notes under their doors. She hoped they would understand . . . and love the idea of being part of the celebration.

When Melli reached the harbor, it was quiet. No other Ice Cream Fairies were there yet. The sunlight glistened on the water like sugar crystals. The sight took her breath away.

"Delicious, right?" Drizzle said as she and Fluff came up behind Melli. "This is the best spot in the isles to see the sunrise."

"In Sugar Valley, Sun Dip is my favorite time of day," Melli said. "The colors of the sky are yummy and I visit with my friends." She turned to look at her new friends. "Here the sunrise is just as sweet. I'm really glad that you and Fluff are here."

Drizzle and Fluff gave Melli a tight squeeze.

"We're so happy you're here and that we became friends," Fluff said.

"This promises to be a *sugar-tastic* day," Drizzle added.

Dips swam up close to the shore. Her white head peeked out above the water. Melli hoped their plan would work! Pulling a large float with seven fairies might not be simple for the small seal.

Melli flew out over the water to greet Dips. She showed the seal the licorice harness and how it should slip over her head.

"I'll hold the reins," she explained. "All you have to do is swim. We don't need to go fast. Let's give it try, okay?"

Dips nodded and slapped her flippers in a playful splash.

Drizzle and Fluff pulled the float closer to

the water's edge. Together, the fairies hooked the reins to the float. Melli held her breath. She stood with Drizzle and Fluff on the float as Dips started to move.

"Hot caramel! She's doing it!" Melli cried. "Are you okay?" she called to Dips.

Dips waved a flipper and continued forward.

Melli was so happy. Dips would be the star of the Spectacular!

"Come on," said Fluff, grinning. "Let's go back to the palace and get your friends."

"Yes, let's," Drizzle said, smiling. "We need to give them a proper welcome to Ice Cream Isles."

"And there is no better way than on a float pulled by a Sweet Cream Harbor seal!" Fluff added.

As the fairies returned to the palace they

saw that it was decorated with many swirls of ice cream and toppings.

Before Melli, Drizzle, and Fluff entered the dining hall, they went to check on the caramel sauce one last time. Melli was so proud. Now everything was set for the celebration.

But Melli was not prepared to be greeted by four very sour faces in the dining hall.

"Where were you?" Dash asked. "We woke up and you were gone."

"We were worried," Raina said.

"And a little mad," Berry said. "We came because we wanted to be with you. You sounded so lonely. But you don't want to be with us at all."

Melli's wings dipped low to the floor. "Oh, sugar sticks," she said. "Not another misunderstanding! Didn't you see my notes? I slipped notes under your bedroom doors before I left this morning. I wanted to surprise you all today. Not make you mad!"

Cocoa stepped forward. "Surprise *us*?" she asked.

"Please don't be mad," Melli said. "I was having a hard time in the beginning. I really should have listened to what you told me before I came here. At first I *was* homesick, but I didn't give my new friends a chance. Once I did, I realized we had a lot in common . . . and we had fun together.

"So much fun that you forgot about us?" Dash asked.

Melli flew over to Dash. "Never!" she shouted. "Our surprise is that you can be a part of the Summer Spectacular! All of you can ride on the ice cream float with me, Drizzle, and Fluff!" Melli exclaimed. "And Dips the seal is going to pull us!"

"Are you joking?" Cocoa asked.

"Sure as sugar, I am absolutely telling the truth," Melli said. "I couldn't be happier that you will be with me. And it was Drizzle and Fluff's idea that you ride with us."

Cocoa stood up. "We were wrong," she admitted. "I guess we felt that if those fairies weren't nice to you, then we wouldn't be nice to them."

"And that was definitely *not* nice," Raina added.

"We should have behaved better," Berry said.

"We should start all over," Dash said.

Drizzle and Fluff flew over. "We'd like that," they said at the same time. "We're sorry too, if Melli felt left out. That was never our intention."

Melli grinned. She was so happy to see all her friends together. A horn blew, and Melli knew it was time to get on the float. They couldn't miss the opening of the great float parade!

The fairies all took their places. Melli could tell that everyone was surprised to see such a large and fairy-filled float!

Along the Sweet Cream Harbor, many fairies cheered as the colorful procession passed. Melli smiled at her new and old friends.

"Sure as sugar, we have the best float," Melli

boasted as they glided around the harbor.

"Look, there are Princess Lolli and Prince Scoop!" Dash exclaimed.

At the front of the lineup, the prince and princess were in a swirled float with colorful sprinkles. The royal couple looked so happy.

"Delicious. Like the cherry on a sundae," Melli said, smiling at her Ice Cream Fairy friends.

After the grand parade, everyone headed to Swirl Island for the ice cream feast. There were so many flavors and colors! The new flavor was a bright pink, and Berry and Cocoa cheered when they realized that the flavor was strawberry-chocolate swirl.

"Pretty and delicious," Berry said.

Melli wasn't sure what to eat first. And there,

in center of the square, was her caramel sauce!

"Melli, this sauce is just what I had imagined for the Spectacular," Prince Scoop said. He was holding a large bowl of ice cream with Melli's sauce. "Thank you! We'll never have this feast again without your special sauce!"

Melli blushed. "It was an honor," she said.

She looked over and saw Raina and Cocoa talking to Drizzle, and Dash and Berry laughing with Fluff. This made Melli grin. It was supersweet when friends blended together. She took a spoonful of her strawberry-chocolate swirl and sighed. She had been so afraid to go on this journey alone, but she had done it! And though it was a little sticky at first, now everything was *sugar-tastic*!

"This trip has been delicious," she said to Prince Scoop. "Thank you again . . . for everything."

As all the fairies settled onto the pier with their ice cream sundaes, Melli sighed. The trip had taught her a good lesson about

traveling and making new friends. This was
a big double scoop of friendship with all the
trimmings—including caramel sauce. She
dipped her spoon in her bowl. It was the
perfect sweet-treat ending to share with new
friends and old.